CONTENTS

PRAYER
SUPPLEMENT

Wale Ola

A Daily Prayer of Dedication and
Declaration of Victory

PRAYER SUPPLEMENT
ISBN 978-0-9573406-2-6
Copyright © Wale Ola

Designed and published in the United Kingdom
by HCL Media

I

INTRODUCTION

"One day Jesus told His disciples a story to show that they should always pray and never give up." (Luke 18:1 NLT)

Prayer though being one of, if not the most potent connector with God that we have as Christians, is nevertheless at the same time, one of the most daunting disciplines that many find quite hard to maintain or practise with any consistency.

As a new believer, one of the most frustrating experiences that I had in those early days, was the confusion about prayer — how to pray, what to pray or when to pray. I thought I did not know enough fancy words to express myself to God or to couch the bucket list of petitions that I wanted to table before Him. That notwithstanding, I still struggled a great deal with running out of words after about 5 minutes, and marvelled at those that said they were able to pray for 30 minutes or more, and saw one hour as an unattainable eternity!

The Bible tells us in the second part of James 5:16 (NLT) that, *"The earnest prayer of a righteous person has great power and produces wonderful results."* That's saying that there is a promise for us believers, that our prayers offered up to God with fervency and persistence, have great power and will produce wonderful results. But right there is the challenge — fervency and consistency!

Wouldn't it be amazing however, if we could walk in the reality of the manifestation of that wonderful promise everyday of our lives?

What I pray that this book will do for you, is to provide a *supplement* to your daily prayers, by highlighting and helping you to articulate 20 different areas you may want to bring before God in your prayer time. It is by no means an exhaustive list, but a foundation that is fully based on scripture and in alignment with the template for praying that Jesus taught the disciples in Matthew 6:9-13.

I believe that this prayer supplement will be a blessing and a benefit to both young and mature believers, helping them to expand their prayer horizon, and also add some consistency and focus to their daily prayer time.

HOW THIS CAME TO BE

I believe it is crucial for me to share how this prayer supplement came to be. On Monday the 31st of July 2017, I had a particularly restless night, in which I had very little, if any sleep through the night. It was one of those situations where you felt uneasy in your spirit, but not being able to put your finger on any particular thing that may be causing the uneasiness.

I had prayed before going to bed, but still found that I couldn't really switch off, and had a fitful "sleep" punctuated by fragmented dreams that played in a loop through the night.

Then something strange happened — there was a crossover or should I say an overlap between dream and reality! I had found myself praying in my dream and the prayers that I was praying segued into my waking state and I continued praying as I was in my dreams. At that point, I felt the Holy Spirit nudge me to pick up my iPad, and I began to write down the prayers as I remembered them! This would continue throughout that day, and the result of my encounter that day, is what gave birth to this prayer supplement.

HOW TO USE THE SUPPLEMENT

This supplement is not a *"prayer book"* that is meant to replace your own private, relational prayer time or conversations with God. Rather, it can be used as a template that provides highlights or a foundation that you can build on, covering some of the most common needs that we may have in our daily walk on this side of eternity.

At the very least, the first time that you read through these prayers, it may be helpful for you to read the scriptures that are included in each section, so you can have a scriptural reference for the prayers that you will be saying. Subsequently, you may then go ahead and read the prayers without re-visiting the scriptures. You may find that on different days and at different seasons of your life, different sections may have more relevance and poignancy to capture your thoughts or prayer needs for those times. It may also be that the prayers might spark something that leads you to address certain issues or pray in particular directions.

As I mostly do, you may pray the prayer points every morning (it takes about 30 minutes reading at a regular pace, or longer if you add your own prayers to the points). You may also choose to break the prayers into two parts and pray morning and evening; and if unable to pray it daily, you may instead start every new week or every new month with it.

Ask for the help of the Holy Spirit before you start praying. Do not just mouth off or merely recite the words as some magical incantations; confess and declare them as the word of God that they are, listening for the Holy Spirit to inspire your prayers as He amplifies what you need to pray to you, in addition to the words that you are reading.

Pray for God to bless and honour the words that you speak and for Him to release His unction on your pronouncements. I have seen the Lord do some miraculous things in my life and for our family as myself and my wife have prayed these prayers. I pray that God will come through for you as well, manifesting the workings of His great power in your life and situation, as your prayer of faith produces the wonderful results that He has promised in the precious Name of Jesus Christ. Amen!

"And we are confident that He hears us whenever we ask for anything that pleases Him. And since we know He hears us when we make our requests, we also know that He will give us what we ask for." (1 John 5:14 -15 NLT)

II

MORE THAN JUST A TITLE

You will notice that almost every section of the prayers that you will be saying in this supplement begins with a reference to God as *"Jehovah"*, with an additional descriptive title in tow. In the Scriptures, God introduced Himself to the children of Israel at different times using different Jehovah titles, which are expressions of His divine nature and His covenant relationship with them, and now by extension with us as well. The name "Jesus" itself, has the root meaning — *"Jehovah is Salvation"*.

Jehovah is translated as *"The Existing One"* or *"Lord."* The root meaning of Jehovah is derived from the Hebrew word "Havah" meaning *"to be"* or *"to exist."* Hence, the reference to God as The *"I Am"*; the *"Self-Existent and Eternal Creator"*, as He revealed Himself to Moses in Exodus 3:14.

Jehovah also means *"to become"* or specifically *"to become known"* — this denotes a God who delights in revealing Himself and making His glory known to His people.

Every time we refer to and proclaim the name Jehovah when we pray, we are declaring and invoking the covenant relationship that we have with God through Christ Jesus — reminding ourselves that we have in that Name, the potent power of a covenant keeping God, who is able to work all things out according to the counsel of His own will!

Every Jehovah name by which God has made Himself known, is a covenant promise that we can claim whenever we approach Him in prayers.

(There's a list on page 16 at the end of this section, of all the Jehovah Names that are used in this supplement, with the relevant scripture references to where they appear in the Bible.)

As New Testament Christians, the greatest "title" that we can ever call or know God by, is "Father". Jesus teaches us to pray by addressing and approaching God as our Father in heaven, and then to "Hallow His Name". To hallow a thing is to make it holy or to separate or set it apart to be exalted as being worthy of absolute honour — to hallow the name of God is to regard Him with complete devotion and incomparable exultation.

However in reality, in the name *"Father"*, we have more than just a title; we have a relational promise of God as our source, our protector, our provider and our keeper — a covenant relationship made possible by the blood that Jesus shed for us on the Cross of Calvary.

That is the strength of conviction that is the bedrock of our faith as we come before Him in prayers everyday — we have a loving, faithful Father who will hear and answer our prayers made to Him in the name of Jesus. (Psalm 65:2; Romans 8:32; 2 Corinthians 1:20)

"Let us therefore come boldly to the throne of grace, that we may obtain mercy and find grace to help at the point of need." (Hebrews 4:16 NKJV)

BIBLE REFERENCES FOR JEHOVAH NAMES

Jehovah Adonai, the Sovereign Lord *(Genesis 15:1-3)*

Jehovah Tsidkenu, the Lord my Righteousness *(Jeremiah 23:6; Jeremiah 33:16)*

Jehovah Rapha *or* **Ropheka**, the Lord God that Heals *(Exodus 15:26)*

Jehovah Shammah, the Lord is There; the God who is ever present *(Ezekiel 48:35)*

Jehovah Nissi, the Lord my Banner *(Exodus 17:15)*

Jehovah Elyon, the Lord, the Most High God *(Gen 14:18-22; Psalm 57:2; Psalm 78:35)*

Jehovah Rohi, the Lord God my Shepherd *(Psalm 23; Psalm 80:1; Ezekiel 34:11-15)*

Jehovah Jireh, the Lord God my provider *(Genesis 22:14)*

Jehovah Elshaddai, the All-Sufficient God *(Genesis 17:1; Genesis 28:3)*

Jehovah Elohim, the All-powerful, Omnipotent One *(Genesis 1:1)*

Jehovah Sabaoth, the Lord of Hosts; God of the Angel Armies *(1 Samuel 1:3; Psalm 24:9-10; Psalm 84:3; Isaiah 6:5)*

Jehovah Shalom, the Lord is Peace *(Judges 6:24)*

Jehovah El-Olam, the God of Eternity, the Everlasting God; God of The Ancient Days (Genesis 21:33; Jeremiah 10:10; Isaiah 26:4)

III

PRAYERS

(If you are saying these prayers at the beginning of a week, month or year, you can substitute "this day" or "today", with "this week", "this month", or "this year")

My dear heavenly Father, I thank You for the gift of life and for the gift of this new day.

I thank You for the gift of salvation and the privilege of being Your child and the access that I have to You through Christ Jesus. (Psalm 100:1-5; Romans 5:1-2; Ephesians 2:13-19)

1 ~ SELF EXAMINATION / CONFESSION OF SINS

I confess and repent of every sin that I have committed, and every act of unrighteousness that has dishonoured Your Name and which the enemy has

used or can use against me, to accuse me
before the courts of heaven today.

I plead the blood of Jesus Christ as I ask
for Your mercy and forgiveness today and
from my heart, I forgive and release
anyone who has offended or hurt me in
anyway. (Psalm 66:18; Mark 11:25-26; 1John 1:8-9)

2 ~ RAISE AN ALTAR OF PRAISE AND WORSHIP UNTO GOD

Almighty God; I acknowledge You as the
Creator and the Possessor of the heavens
and the earth. (Hebrews 11:4)

You are the Omnipotent, yet gracious
and merciful God, who does awesome
things in righteousness. I worship Your
majesty today as I bow down in humble
adoration before Your throne of grace. I
come to You in the name of Your dear
Son Jesus Christ who I confess and
declare to be the Messiah, my Saviour
and my Lord. I raise an altar unto You in
the name of my Lord and Saviour Jesus
Christ.

By the workings and speakings of the blood that Jesus shed for me on the Cross of Calvary, I present myself to you on that altar as a living sacrifice, and I bring my sacrifice of praise, worship and thanksgiving to You. (Hebrews 13:8-15)

(You can pause for a session of praise and worship)

You are Alpha and Omega, the first and the last, the beginning and the ending, the Maker and Possessor of the heavens and the earth. You are the Mighty Man of war; the first and the only Potentate, the One and only true and living God! You O Lord, are the One who alone is deserving of all the praise, all the worship and all my adoration.

3 ~ DEDICATION / SUBMISSION TO GOD'S WILL

You are *Jehovah Adonai*, the Sovereign Lord! Let Your kingdom come and let Your will alone be done in my life today.

My precious heavenly Father, I dedicate

and consecrate myself to You in the name of Jesus. I dedicate and consecrate all that I have to You — my spouse, my children, my home my household, my entire family and all that we possess.

I dedicate and consecrate my substance to You — I dedicate my finances, my ministry, my business, my job and my house to You. Let them all be used for Your glory.

I dedicate and consecrate my body to You — let it be Your holy temple in which You are pleased to dwell. Let my life be conformed to the image of Jesus Christ my Lord. (Romans 12:1-2)

I renounce every ungodly and contrary covenant that is in existence in or over my life, in my neighbourhood or in my heritage *(mention your own nationality or nationalities and place / state of origin here — e.g. British and Nigerian, American and Indian, etc)*, and I remove myself and my family from any and every ungodly covenants that I have ever entered into or any that were made on our behalf by any person or people dead or alive.

I release myself and my family from the demands, consequences and influence of every such covenants and vows in our lives in the name of Jesus Christ.

I silence the voices speaking from every demonic or satanic altar, against me and my family and all that concerns us, in the name of Jesus.

4 ~ BREAK CURSES/EVIL PRONOUNCEMENTS

You are *Jehovah Tsidkenu*, the Lord my Righteousness. I agree with, and declare Your word that says that I am Your righteousness in Christ Jesus.

I declare that no weapon that is formed against me shall prosper, and every tongue that rises against me in judgement is condemned in the name Of Jesus — This is my covenant heritage as Your child. (Jeremiah 23:5-6; 2 Corinthians 5:21; Isaiah 54:17)

In the mighty name of our Lord and Saviour Jesus Christ, I cancel every curse and every evil pronouncements that have been issued or spoken against us and our destinies. (Lamentations 3:37)

I break myself and my family free from the power and influence of every curse or divination or enchantment in the name of Jesus.

In the name of Jesus, I bind and remove from my life and my family, every strongman and satanic agents or demonic agencies that the enemy has assigned to enforce a curse or evil pronouncements or satanic orders over our lives and destiny. (Mark 3:27; Luke 11:21-22)

I forbid them in the name of Jesus, from interfering with any area of our lives and from afflicting or oppressing us in any way.

I command in the name of Jesus Christ, that the operations and effects of such evil utterances and satanic transactions over our lives come to an end and cease to manifest with immediate effect.

5 ~ DIVINE HEALTH/HEALING

I bless Your Holy Name, *Jehovah Rapha* — the Lord God my Healer. You have promised in Your word, that You will bless our bread and our water, and take sickness away from our midst. Your word also declares that I am healed by the stripes of Christ.

I invoke and claim this covenant promise of divine health in the name of Jesus.

I rebuke the spirit of infirmity in the name of Jesus. I rebuke every sickness or symptom of ill health in my life and in the lives of every member of my family *(and church)* in the name of Jesus Christ.

Because of the effectual working of the completed works of Christ on the Cross of Calvary and the power in His shed blood speaking on our behalf, I remove myself and every member of my family from any sickness or malaise that exists or is prevalent in our blood line.

Jehovah Ropheka, let Your healing power be released to flow through and saturate every area of my life right this moment — let it touch spirit, soul and body, to heal me and my family, where there is any sickness or disease, whether physical, emotional, mental, psychological or spiritual; whether known or unknown, and to keep us in good, sound, divine health, as You have promised.

Whatever areas of my life are broken, damaged or infirmed, I receive healing and wholeness and complete liberty from every oppression of the enemy in Jesus' name. (Isaiah 53:5; 1 Peter 2:24; Exodus 23:25-26)

6 ~ EVIDENCE / MANIFESTATION OF GOD'S PRESENCE

I worship You Almighty God — I acknowledge You as *Jehovah Shammah*, the God who is ever present. I pray dear Lord, that Your holy presence will be with me everywhere that I go today, that I will host and carry the presence of Your glory with me in every place that I am. (Exodus 33:13-17; 2 Corinthians 2:14)

I expect and declare that today, the tangible evidence of Your manifest presence will be visible and acknowledged in every area of my life — in my home, in my ministry, in my business, in everything that I do.

As Your word declares, I will know and live in the fullness of joy and the pleasures that manifest with Your presence in my life today in the name of Jesus. (Psalm 16:11)

Let my life bring pleasure to You today; let it bring honour and praise to Your Name as You use me for Your glory in the name of Jesus. (Revelations 4:9-11)

7 ~ DIVINE PROTECTION AND VICTORY

You are *Jehovah Nissi*; the Lord my Banner,

my defender and my victory! (Deuteronomy 33:26-28)

I surrender to the reign and rule of Your kingdom over every area of my life. I dedicate and consecrate this day to You — everywhere I go and everything that I do. I bring every moment of this day, together with everything that concerns me today, under the influence and dominion of Your kingdom. (Ephesians 1:15-23)

8 ~ ACTIVATION OF COVENANT BLESSINGS

You are *Jehovah Elyon*; the Lord, the Most High God — the One from whom all blessings flow. (Genesis 14:19-20; Ephesians 1:3)

I invoke and activate every blessing of the covenant that I have with You in Christ Jesus. I release them and walk in the fullness of these blessings from this day.

I pray Lord, that every area of my life will begin to manifest and reflect these blessings today, to the praise and glory of Your Holy Name.

I declare that because this is the day that You Lord have made I will rejoice and be glad in it. I declare that the heavens are open over me and unto me today for the benefits and blessings of the Covenant to locate me and be released into my life today in the name of Jesus.

I ask Lord in the name of Jesus, that because I live and walk under open heavens as Christ has said, that You open the floodgates of heaven and send Your rain of abundance over my life and over the land upon which I walk, and that the earth will yield its increase unto me today. (Psalm 67:1-7)

I ask You dear Father, the benevolent and gracious God, that in the name of Jesus, You will bless me indeed today.

I receive all that I need to prosper and fulfil Your assignment for my life today for the advancement of Your kingdom, and for the fulfilment of Your call upon my life, and the destiny that You have ordained for me.

I declare that from this day, in the name of Jesus Christ, I will no longer labour in vain nor will I toil for no reward or minimum returns! (Isaiah 62:8-9)

9 ~ ENFORCEMENT OF CALVARY'S VICTORY

I claim and enforce the victory that Christ won for me on the cross of Calvary, over every area of my life.

I therefore remove this day and all that it holds, from the dominion and influence of the powers of darkness in the name of Jesus — I remove myself and my family, I remove all that we have, and the works of our hands.

I remove my home, I remove my ministry, I remove my business, I remove my job, I remove my career, I remove my working environment, I remove my finances and my wealth, and I bring them all under the authority and dominion of the power of the kingdom of Jehovah, the Most High God. (Colossians1:13; Colossians 2:14-15)

I pray for the unsaved in my family and in the nations that the veil will be taken off of their minds so they may come to know Jesus Christ as their Lord and Saviour. (2 Corinthians 4:3-4; Luke 15:7; 1 Timothy 2:3)

I pray also for the leaders of this nation, the community that I live in and the establishment that I am a part of *(mention your church, work or school)* that they will align with, and surrender to the will of God, and make righteous judgements and decisions in their governance, to favour the welfare of God's Kingdom, and to agree with Your counsel for my family and myself, in the name of Jesus. (1 Timothy 2:1-4)

10 ~ GOD'S GUIDANCE/LEADING

You are *Jehovah Rohi* — the Lord God my Shepherd, and because of this, I will not lack for any good thing. (Psalm 23:1)

You have said in Your word that the steps of the righteous are ordered by You. Order my steps today O Lord, lead me along the paths that You have chosen for me and let Your glory be seen in me, as I journey through life. (Psalm 32:8)

I pray dear Lord, that You will keep me from falling and that my faith will not fail; keep me also Lord from every evil, and keep every evil away from me. (Jude 1:24-25; Psalm 37:23-25; John 16:13-14)

11 ~ FRESH ANOINTING OF THE HOLY SPIRIT

I receive a fresh infilling of the Holy Spirit and surrender to His promptings and complete influence over my life.

I petition You Lord, to please activate and release the anointing — the unction of the Holy Spirit over my life, my family, my household, my ministry, my job and over my business, to lift every burden and to destroy every yoke in the precious name of Jesus Christ. (Zechariah 4:6-7; 2 Corinthians 3:17)

According to the words of Christ in Luke 4:18-19; let there be an activation and release in my life, of the anointing for breakthroughs for myself *(in my ministry, in my job/business)*; in my family, and in the lives and situations of all those that I will pray for or minister to today, in the mighty name of Jesus. (Ephesians 6:18-19; Colossians 4:2-3)

I activate and release every natural gift, abilities and talents, and every Spiritual blessing that I have been given in Christ Jesus. *(Mention your children's names here and pray this over their lives, especially if you have young children.)* I also ask dear Father in the name of Jesus, that You activate and release every gift of the Holy Spirit that I need for ministry today. (Ephesians 1:3; 1 Corinthians 12:4-31; Ephesians 4:7-11)

As You have said in Your word, let my gifts and Your grace upon my life, position me in the place of favour, promotion and honour; let them bring me before kings and people of influence, and let them make room for my advancement today, as You locate me by Your divine providence and You position me through divinely orchestrated appointments, in the places of my blessings and breakthroughs in Jesus' name. (Proverbs 18:16)

12 ~ DIVINE FAVOUR

I receive FAVOUR and the GRACE to walk in VICTORY and to PROSPER. I therefore command the doors of divine favour to open unto me today in the name of Jesus.

I pray for the doors of effective ministry, even to the nations, to open unto me today.

I will find and receive mercy and help; kindness and favour will be shown and given to me and my family everywhere we go and everywhere our names are mentioned today in the name of Jesus. (Psalm 102:13; Philippians 4:19)

13 ~ DIVINE PROVISION AND SUSTENANCE

Because I walk and live in the grace of my Lord Jesus Christ, I bind and reject the spirit of poverty and lack from my life in the name of Jesus. I claim the riches and blessings of Your grace upon my life as a result of the divine exchange that was made on my behalf on the Cross of Calvary. (2 Corinthians 8:9)

I call on Your name *Jehovah Jireh*, You are the Lord God my provider. I pray for the release, and I receive all the provisions and resources that are required for me to live the abundant life that Christ has promised me and for me to prosper in the fullness of the call upon my life. (John 10:10; Philippians 4:19)

I call on Your name *Jehovah Elshaddai*, You are the All sufficient God. You are my Sufficiency!

Dear Lord, in response to Your invitation to me in Hebrews 4:16, I petition You for the release and I receive supernatural financial resources and material provisions to meet every need and obligations that are due today and in this season of my life.

In the name of Jesus Christ, I pray Lord that I will have an abundance and overflow of blessings, enough for me to be a blessing to the work of Your Kingdom, to my local church, to my family, to other people, and even to the nations. (2 Corinthians 9:6-15; Genesis 12:2)

14 ~ FRUITFULNESS

Lord Jesus, You said in Your Word, that You called and chose me to bear enduring fruit and to live an abundant life. (John 15:16; John 10:10)

Therefore in agreement with Your will for my life, I bind and rebuke the spirit of death and barrenness from my life, from my ministry and from my business and I speak and command fruitfulness as God intends, into every area of my life in Jesus' name. (Exodus 23:25; Ezekiel 47:6-12)

I call on Your name *Jehovah Elohim*, The all-powerful, Omnipotent One, to cause the heavens and the earth and all that they hold and contain to work together on my behalf and favour me this day.

15 ~ ANGELIC ASSISTANCE / MINISTRATION

I ask O Sovereign Lord, You who are *Jehovah Sabaoth*, the Lord of Hosts — God of the angel armies, that You will release and assign Your angels to work on my behalf today.

Therefore, by faith in Your word, I activate and welcome the assistance and ministry of Your angelic hosts in my life today in the name of Jesus Christ. (Hebrews 1:14; Acts 12:5-11)

16 ~ DIVINE WISDOM

I receive the Spirit of wisdom and revelation in the knowledge of God.

I ask dear Lord, for divine wisdom to unlock the solution to every problem and the answer to every question that today will bring — I receive divine wisdom to make the right choices and the correct decisions today, by the divine inspiration and counsel of Your Holy Spirit. (Job 32:8; Proverbs 8:12; James 1:5; Ephesians 1:15-23)

I receive the knowledge of witty inventions and the power to get wealth.

17 ~ DIVINE HELP/HONOUR/ PROMOTION

I release and receive the divine helpers that You Jehovah have ordained to be a support and blessing to my life — the help providers for the fulfilment of my destiny, and that of my spouse, my children, my family; I release the divine helpers for my ministry, my job, and my business, in the name of Jesus.

In the name of Jesus, I bind and remove from my life today, every strongman and satanic agents or demonic agencies that the enemy has assigned to hinder my progress, or to resist or prevent my provisions or my helpers and their help from reaching me or my family or household, in our time of need, or in any area or season of our lives *(In our Church, ministry, business, work, career, finances, etc)*.

I command the ancient gates to open for my supplies to reach me today. I command the heavenly and earthly gateways and storehouses of blessings and divine sustenance to be open and available to me and my household today in the name of Jesus. (Isaiah 60:11; Psalm 24:1-10)

I pray dear Heavenly Father, that You will cause the doors of divine opportunities, doors of honour, promotion and influence to be open unto me today in the name of Jesus. (Revelations 3:7)

18 ~ GOD'S PEACE / DIVINE ALIGNMENT

I acknowledge You as *Jehovah Shalom*, the Lord God of My Peace. I enter into Your rest today, together with every member of my family and household.

I call upon every area of my life and endeavours today, to align with Your word, plans and counsel concerning me and my destiny; I speak Your peace, the peace of Christ into every area of my life today. (Isaiah 59:19; Isaiah 54:14; John 14:27)

I speak to, and command every storm and contrary winds that are raging or brewing in my life; my home, my work or in the ministry, Peace be still! In the name of Jesus!

I pray for the peace of this nation that I live in, and I pray for the peace of Jerusalem. (Jeremiah 29:7; Psalm 122:6)

19 ~ DIVINE RESTORATION

In the name of Jesus, I declare that there will be restoration today in my life — in my family, my business and in my ministry, of all that has been lost, stolen, or withheld, and the years that have been wasted and devoured by the enemy.

I declare in the name of Jesus, that from today, the cycle of losses, delays, disappointments, barrenness and defeat have come to an end in my life and I enter into a never-ending cycle of divine favour, blessings, fruitfulness and victory. (2 Corinthians 2:14)

My times are in Your hands O Lord, You are the Lord who is the Creator and Controller of time. You are the Self-Existent and Eternal Creator who exists outside of time and is not limited by the constraints of times or seasons. (Psalm 31:15)

I pray today O Lord, that You will restore the years, redeem the time and restore the seasons of my life in accordance with the timings of Your plans, and in agreement with Your agenda and divine purpose for my destiny. (Joel 2:23-27; Zechariah 8:1-23)

Heavenly Father, I pray also, that You will even cause lost, denied or wasted opportunities that were meant for my promotion and progress, and the fulfilment of Your counsel for my life and Your plans for my destiny, to be fully restored unto me today, in the name of Jesus Christ.

As Jeremiah says in Jeremiah 20:11, I also declare: *"But the Lord is with me as a mighty, awesome One. Therefore my persecutors will stumble, and will not prevail. They will be greatly ashamed, for they will not prosper. Their everlasting confusion will never be forgotten."* (NKJV)

Again I declare according to Your word in Isaiah 8:10, If they take counsel together against us, it will come to nothing; if they speak any contrary word, it will not stand, for You O God are with us.

For there is no one like You our God. You who rides across the heavens to help us, across the skies in majestic splendour. You are the Eternal God who is our refuge, and Your everlasting arms are under us. You drive out the enemy before us; crying out, "Destroy them!" So we will live in safety, in prosperity and security, in a land of plenty, while the heavens drop down dew. (Deuteronomy 33:26-28 paraphrased)

Because Christ became a curse for me on the Cross of Calvary and redeemed me by the blood of His Sacrifice, I have passed from death into abundant life, and from curses into blessings in Him. (Colossians 1:13; Colossians 2:13-15; Galatians 3:13-14)

(Spend some time to listen to the Holy Spirit before closing — there may be something that God wants to say to you in response to your prayers — someone to intercede for, a particular situation to pray about, or instructions for you to obey.)

20 ~ THANKSGIVING

Jehovah El-Olam, the God of Eternity, the Everlasting God; the faithful God, the God of unsearchable counsel and immutable covenants! You are the King immortal, the King invincible, the only wise God, the One who alone is truly deserving and worthy of all my praise and worship!

I believe Your word that declares that every promise of Yours to me are Yes and Amen in Christ Jesus. I therefore thank you heavenly Father, for hearing and answering my prayers today in Jesus' name. (Psalm 65:2; Romans 8:32; John 16:24, 2 Corinthians 1:20, Philippians 4:6-8)

Amen!

IV

FINAL WORD

PRAYER OF SALVATION

If you are reading this and have never made a personal commitment to Jesus by asking Him to be your Saviour and Lord, the prayer of salvation is the most important prayer you will ever pray in your life. (John 3:3)

Salvation is a free gift that God has made available to you in Christ Jesus. To avail yourself of this gift, all you have to do is confess your sins and accept the sacrifice that Jesus made on your behalf of the Cross of Calvary, and invite Him to be your Saviour and your Lord. (Ephesians 2:8-9)

The Bible tells us that it is appointed for man to die once and then judgement. But for the sacrifice that Jesus made for us on Calvary's Cross by shedding His blood as an atonement for our sins, we are all condemned to an eternity in hell. The word of God however assures us, that if we confess Jesus as Lord with our mouth and believe it in our hearts, we shall be saved. (Hebrews 9:27-28; 2 Corinthians 5:21; John 3:16; Romans 10:5-13)

Here's an invitation for you to pray this prayer of salvation and become born again and a part of God's family. Please say this prayer with belief and conviction in your heart to receive this precious gift:

Dear Heavenly Father, I thank You for sending Your Son Jesus Christ to die for my sins on the Cross. I confess my sins and I ask for Your forgiveness as I come to You in repentance today.

I accept the sacrifice that Jesus made on my behalf on the cross and I believe that You raised Him up from the dead to save me.

I ask You dear Jesus, to come into my heart and be my Saviour and my Lord.I commit my life to You from this moment, and ask that through the help of Your Holy Spirit,

You will empower me to live for You for the rest of my days. Amen!

If you've prayed this prayer of salvation with true conviction and sincerity, you are now a follower of Jesus. Please look for a Bible believing, Spirit-Filled church to join, and let them know that you've prayed this prayer of salvation and would love to know more about the commitment that you have made.

Lightning Source UK Ltd.
Milton Keynes UK
UKHW022103260121
377710UK00006B/22